# Jenny Found a Penny

To Holly, Mark, Andrew, Julie, and Emily. You're priceless!
—T.H.

For Amy
—J.H.

Millbrook Press, Inc.
A division of Lerner Publishing Group, Inc.
241 First Avenue North
Minneapolis, MN 55401 U.S.A.

Website address: www.lernerbooks.com

Library of Congress Cataloging-in-Publication Data

Harris, Trudy.
  Jenny found a penny / by Trudy Harris ; illustrated by John Hovell.
      p.   cm.
  Summary: The reader can help Jenny count her pennies—and nickels and dimes and quarters—
as she saves the money to buy herself a very special present.
  ISBN: 978–0–8225–6725–7 (lib. bdg. : alk. paper)
  [1. Saving and investment—Fiction. 2. Stories in rhyme.]  I. Hovell, John, ill.  II. Title.
PZ8.3.H24318Je  2008
[E]—dc22                                                                                    2006100299

Manufactured in the United States of America
1 2 3 4 5 6 – JR – 13 12 11 10 09 08

# Jenny Found a Penny

**Trudy Harris**

illustrations by **John Hovell**

Ⓜ Millbrook Press · Minneapolis

# Jenny found a penny

in the backseat of the car.
She put that shiny penny
in an empty pickle jar.

One penny—worth one cent—
into the pickle jar it went.

Jenny found four pennies
underneath her mother's bed.
She gave them to her mother.
Mom said, "Keep them all instead."

One penny,
plus these four—
that made five.
She needed more.

Jenny earned two nickels
when she babysat her brothers.
She dropped both coins into the jar
along with all the others.

Two nickels—
five cents each—
still her goal was not in reach.

Jenny earned a silver dime
for helping Grandpa J.
She swept the porch and sidewalk
and put the broom away.

Ten cents in a dime—
would she reach
her goal in time?

Jenny got a quarter,
a gift from Uncle Ned.
"Spend your money wisely,"
was all her uncle said.

Twenty-five cents more to add
to the money that she had.

Jenny earned a half-dollar,
and by her account,
fifty cents (with all the rest)
made just the right amount.

Finally, she'd succeeded.
She had the cash she needed.

$.01
.04
.05
.05
.10
.25
.50

$1.00

Jenny and her sister, Kate,
walked to the dollar store.
Jenny knew what she would buy.
She'd seen it twice before.

One was left—high on the shelf.
Jenny reached it by herself.

Jenny gave her money
to the dollar-store cashier,
but the lady shook her head and said,
"You've got a problem here.

This total somehow lacks
seven cents to pay the tax."

Jenny felt like crying
as she headed for the door.
She'd worked and saved her money,
but still, she needed more.

Then,
like an awful curse,
her troubles went
from bad to worse.

Jenny tripped and stumbled,
and her feet flew in the air.
The bottle slipped. It cracked and chipped,
and coins spilled everywhere.

By the counter,
on the floor,

in the entry,
out the door,

on the sidewalk,
near the street,

kicked by people's
passing feet.

Jenny and her sister
picked up every coin they could,
but Kate told Jenny she was sure
that some were lost for good.
Kate said, "Do your best,
and we'll have to leave the rest."

Jenny gathered up the change
to count it one last time,
but something very strange occurred....
She had an EXTRA dime!

On her way back home that day, she danced a happy jig.

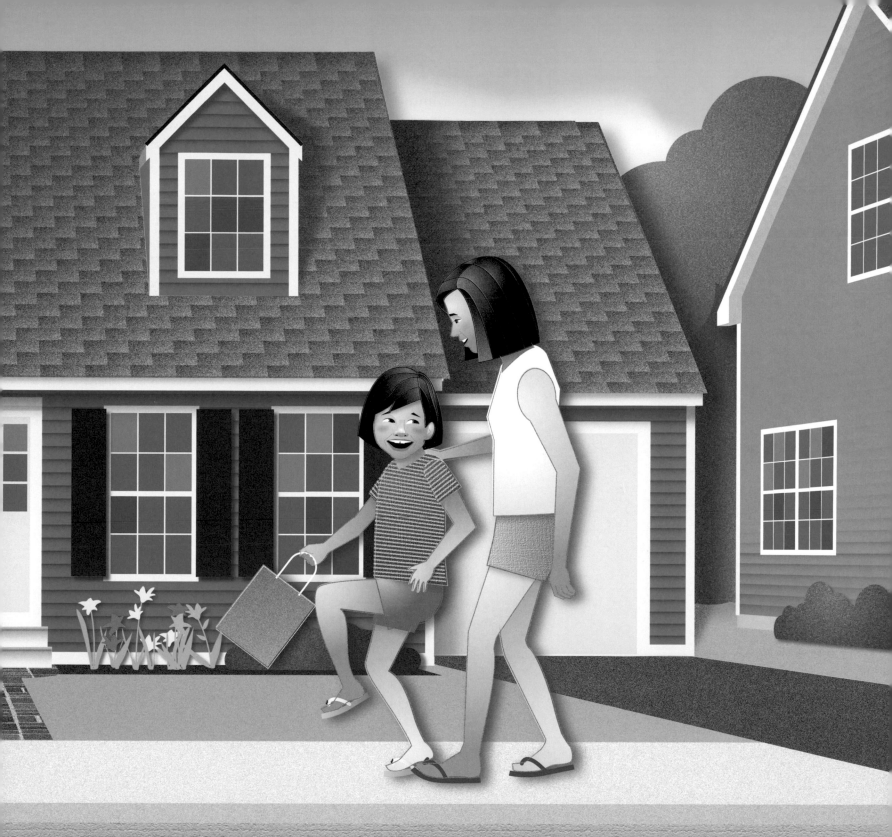

Then Jenny put three pennies . . .

in her brand-new plastic pig.